Groundwood Books / House of Anansi Press
110 Spadina Avenue, Suite 801, Toronto, Ontario M5V 2K4
or c/o Publishers Group West
1700 Fourth Street, Berkeley, CA 94710

We acknowledge for their financial support of our publishing program
the Canada Council for the Arts, the Government of Canada through the
Canada Book Fund (CBF) and the Ontario Arts Council.

 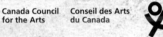

Library and Archives Canada Cataloguing in Publication
Kulling, Monica, author
Grant and Tillie go walking / written by Monica Kulling ; illustrated
by Sydney Smith.
Issued in print and electronic formats.
ISBN 978-1-55498-446-6 (bound).—ISBN 978-1-55498-448-0 (pdf)
1. Wood, Grant, 1891-1942—Juvenile fiction.
I. Smith, Sydney, illustrator II. Title.
PS8571.U54G74 2015   jC813'.54   C2015-900026-2
C2015-900027-0

The illustrations were done using watercolors, ink and a toothbrush.
Design by Michael Solomon
Printed and bound in Malaysia

For Sheila Barry — MK

To Alexandra, Mica, Sadie and Peter.
My oldest and youngest friends. — SS

I realized that all the really good ideas I'd ever
had came to me while I was milking a cow.
So I went back to Iowa. — GRANT WOOD

GRANT
and
TILLIE
Go Walking

PICTURES BY

MONICA KULLING   SYDNEY SMITH

GROUNDWOOD BOOKS   HOUSE OF ANANSI PRESS   TORONTO   BERKELEY

GRANT WOOD was walking down the road with Tillie. The Brown Swiss cow had a face as sweet as sunrise and a smile as gentle as the nearby rolling hills.

Once in a while, Tillie stopped to graze on tufts of grass. She was a happy cow.

Grant Wood was not happy. He gazed at the hills, winding roads, and fields of corn and wheat. He longed for more excitement.

Tillie was born on the farm. She had never thought of living anyplace else.

At milking time, Tillie gave Grant gallons of frothy goodness. They say that cows with names give more milk, and Tillie gave all she had, morning and night.

Grant was born on the farm too, but deep down he knew
he did not want to be a farmer. Grant wanted to be an artist.
He drew what he saw — barns, barrows, chickens and cows.

Relaxing under an apple tree, Tillie felt the sun warm her sleek brown back. She picked up an apple and dropped it into Grant's open palm. What a cow!

Grant chewed the apple while Tillie chewed her cud.

"I'm leaving for Paris tomorrow, Miss Tillie," Grant said. "I want to paint like the French artists do."

Tillie's brow furrowed. She didn't like the sound of that.

It was the summer of 1920. The city of Paris was lit up like fireworks.

"No wonder they call it the City of Lights!" exclaimed Marvin, Grant's friend and fellow painter.

There was a tower that looked like an iron bridge to the sky. It was named after the man who built it — Eiffel.

Tourists took an elevator to the top of the tower to get a bird's-eye view. From up high, Paris looked like a sparkling diamond necklace.

In Paris, Grant wore city clothes instead of overalls. He wore a French cap, called a beret, and grew a beard. He stayed up late in cafés, drinking and talking with other artists.

If the folks in Iowa could see him now, they wouldn't recognize him. He barely recognized himself!

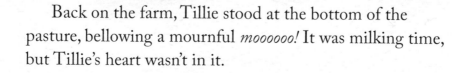

Back on the farm, Tillie stood at the bottom of the
pasture, bellowing a mournful *moooooo!* It was milking time,
but Tillie's heart wasn't in it.

Poor Tillie wasn't giving gallons of milk anymore. One or two pints were all she could muster.

Grant's mother tried to cheer her up by making Tillie's favorite oatmeal mush. Tillie sniffed it, but couldn't eat one bite.

Grant and Marvin painted outdoors. They attacked their canvases with brushes and palette knives. Their lines were bold and bright, and their paintings unlike anything they had painted before.

Marvin's paintings sold quickly, but people took one look at Grant's and shook their heads or laughed out loud.

Tillie no longer went walking. Grant's mother didn't think you needed to walk a cow.

"Go on, Miss Tillie," she'd say each morning, giving the cow a soft slap on the backside. "Get some exercise."

But Tillie didn't know which paths to take without Grant. She just stood there and looked down the road.

Grant looked different, but inside he was still a shy,
quiet man, and a slow painter.

"You need to pick up your pace," encouraged Marvin.

Marvin often finished a painting in the morning and
sold it in the afternoon. Sometimes the paint was even a
bit damp!

But it wasn't Grant's way to rush a painting.

One day, a woman stopped to look at Grant's work.

"What is it?" she asked, in French.

Grant's French wasn't the best, but he knew the word for "cow."

"Une vache," he replied.

The woman left, shaking her head and chuckling. The painting didn't look much like a cow at all.

Tillie was getting thin. She gave little milk now.
"What can we do?" Grant's mother asked in despair.
Grant's sister, Nan, sadly shook her head. She had
no idea.

Grant had a dream. In it, the fields and farms of Iowa glowed in the sun and Grant walked the country roads with Tillie. How he missed that cow!

Grant woke from his dream knowing he was going home.

Heading westward on a train, the farms and fields outside his window made his heart sing.

When Tillie saw Grant, she galloped across the field, bawling as she ran, *"Mooooo!"*

"Moo to you too, Miss Tillie," said Grant, hugging the gentle cow's neck. "I'm home."

One morning, Grant was walking down the road with Tillie. They stopped at a white farmhouse with an arched window. Suddenly, Grant had an inspiration.

The next day, he asked Nan and the family's dentist to pose for him in front of the window. The dentist held a pitchfork. No one smiled.

Grant took all the time he needed to make the painting. He wanted to show the world the place he loved and the people he knew best.

When he was finished, he was happy. And when Grant was happy, Tillie was happy too.

The painter Grant Wood was born on his parents' farm in 1891 in Anamosa, Iowa. When Grant was ten, his father died, and Grant moved with his mother and sister to the nearby city of Cedar Rapids.

Grant was a talented artist from a young age. "My first studio was underneath the oval dining-room table, which was covered with a red checkered cloth," he said. As Grant got older, he worried about whether an American from the Midwest could ever be considered a "real" artist. In those days, European painters were called "the Masters." Their way of painting and what they chose to paint was considered fine art.

In the summer of 1920, Grant Wood traveled to Europe with his friend Marvin Cone. He wanted to see the European masterpieces for himself. After only a few months, Grant realized that he had to paint subjects he cared about. And mostly, he cared about the people and places he had grown up with.

I've imagined Grant returning to the farm, although in fact he returned to Cedar Rapids. The farm symbolizes Grant's connection to the countryside he knew and loved, a connection that can be seen in all his later work.

I'm pretty sure that Grant Wood did not own a cow named Tillie. I made her up! However, it is true that Grant said that all his really good ideas came to him while he was milking a cow. Artists often get good ideas while doing something routine like milking a cow, washing the dishes or walking the dog.

American Gothic was exhibited in 1930, winning a prize and bringing Grant Wood instant fame. People disagreed about what the painting meant. Some said Grant was praising country folks. Others thought that Grant was showing how narrow-minded country people could be. Whatever you may think about *American Gothic*, one thing is true — the painting is Grant Wood's greatest achievement.